g
y.
ng!

_our child get there. The program offers
five steps to reading success. Each step includes fun stories and colorful
art or photographs. In addition to original fiction and books with favorite
characters, there are Step into Reading Non-Fiction Readers, Phonics Readers
and Boxed Sets, Sticker Readers, and Comic Readers—a complete literacy
program with something to interest every child.

Learning to Read, Step by Step!

Ready to Read   Preschool–Kindergarten
• big type and easy words • rhyme and rhythm • picture clues
For children who know the alphabet and are eager to
begin reading.

Reading with Help   Preschool–Grade 1
• basic vocabulary • short sentences • simple stories
For children who recognize familiar words and sound out
new words with help.

Reading on Your Own   Grades 1–3
• engaging characters • easy-to-follow plots • popular topics
For children who are ready to read on their own.

Reading Paragraphs   Grades 2–3
• challenging vocabulary • short paragraphs • exciting stories
For newly independent readers who read simple sentences
with confidence.

Ready for Chapters   Grades 2–4
• chapters • longer paragraphs • full-color art
For children who want to take the plunge into chapter books
but still like colorful pictures.

STEP INTO READING® is designed to give every child a successful
reading experience. The grade levels are only guides; children will progress
through the steps at their own speed, developing confidence in their reading.

Remember, a lifetime love of reading starts with a single step!

Step into Reading, Random House, and the Random House colophon are registered trademarks of Penguin Random House LLC.

Visit us on the Web!
StepIntoReading.com
rhcbooks.com

Educators and librarians, for a variety of teaching tools, visit us at RHTeachersLibrarians.com

ISBN 978-0-7364-4254-1 (trade) — ISBN 978-0-7364-9009-2 (lib. bdg.)
ISBN 978-0-7364-4255-8 (ebook)

Printed in the United States of America
10 9 8 7 6 5 4 3 2 1

DISNEY
Stitch

Stitch Goes to School

by John Edwards

illustrated by the Disney Storybook Art Team

Random House 🏠 New York

It is Pet Day at school.

Lilo is taking

Stitch to her class.

They are both excited!

"Time for school!"
Nani cries.
Lilo and Stitch
hurry down the stairs.

Nani tells Stitch

to be good.

He cannot make a mess

or be bad at school.

Everyone brought
a pet to class.
There are dogs,
cats, and turtles.

Stitch sees

the class pet.

It is a frog.

His name is Mr. Phibbs.

Stitch lifts the top
to get a closer look.
Mr. Phibbs hops
out of his tank!

Stitch chases Mr. Phibbs.
They run out
of the classroom
and through the halls.

Stitch finds Mr. Phibbs.

He is in science class.

Stitch joins the class.

He loves science!

Stitch makes smelly smoke!
The students run
from the room.
Mr. Phibbs hops
away, too.

FETERIA

Mr. Phibbs is in
the lunchroom.
Stitch tries to catch him.
He makes a mess instead.

Food fight!

Stitch and Mr. Phibbs

rush out the door.

Stitch chases Mr. Phibbs
through the school.
He goes to art class
and math class.
Stitch learns a lot!

Stitch finally catches
Mr. Phibbs
in gym class.

Stitch makes it back
to class just in time.
It is Lilo's turn to show
the class her pet!

"Stitch is my best friend
and part of my family,"
Lilo says.

She hugs Stitch.

Nani comes to get

Lilo and Stitch after school.

Lilo tells Nani that

Stitch was very good.

Nani buys them all
some ice cream.
What a great
school day!

5